Light Makes Colors

by Jennifer Boothroyd

Lerner Publications Company · Minneapolis

Expand learning beyond the printed book. Download free, complementary educational resources for this book from our website, www.lernerresource.com.

Copyright © 2015 by Lerner Publishing Group, Inc.

All rights reserved. International copyright secured. No part of this book may be reproduced, stored in a retrieval system, or transmitted in any form or by any means—electronic, mechanical, photocopying, recording, or otherwise—without the prior written permission of Lerner Publishing Group, Inc., except for the inclusion of brief quotations in an acknowledged review.

Photos in this book used with the permission of: © venturecx/iStock/Thinkstock, p. 4; © iStockphoto.com/idambies, p. 5; © Jupiterimages/Goodshoot/Thinkstock, p. 6; © Wiskerke/Alamy, p. 7; © Gennadiy Poznyakov/iStock/Thinkstock, p. 8; © iStockphoto.com/cristani, p. 9; © moodboard/Thinkstock, p. 10; © iStockphoto.com/Yuri_Arcurs, p. 11; © targovcom/iStock/Thinkstock, p. 12; © Buzzshotz/Alamy, p. 13; © Tatyana Aleksandrova/iStock/Thinkstock, p. 14; © iStockphoto.com/jophil, p. 15; © Ingram Publishing/Thinkstock, p. 16; © Galyna Andrushko/Hemera/Thinkstock, p. 17; © Biletskiy_Evgeniy/iStock/Thinkstock, p. 18; © Nnerida/iStock/Thinkstock, p. 19; © Christina Hanck/iStock/Thinkstock, p. 20; © iStockphoto.com/kali9, p. 21; © Pete Spiro/Shutterstock.com, p. 22.

Front Cover: © iStockphoto.com/sassy1902

Main body text set in ITC Avant Garde Gothic Std Medium 21/25.
Typeface provided by Adobe Systems.

Lerner Publications Company
A division of Lerner Publishing Group, Inc.
241 First Avenue North
Minneapolis, MN 55401 USA

For reading levels and more information, look up this title at www.lernerbooks.com.

Library of Congress Cataloging-in-Publication Data

Cataloging-in-Publication Data for *Light Makes Colors* is on file at the Library of Congress.
ISBN: 978–1–4677–3914–6 (LB)
ISBN: 978–1–4677–4685–4 (EB)

Manufactured in the United States of America
1 – CG – 7/15/14

Table of Contents

Light Has Color   4

We See Colors   9

Colors All Around   15

Glossary   23

Index   24

Light Has Color

Light makes the **colors** we see.

White light comes from the sun.

White light also comes from lightbulbs.

Light has seven main colors.

White light is made of many different colors.

We see some of light's colors.

We See Colors

Light **reflects** off an object.

Our eyes catch the reflected light. This is how we see.

Objects reflect only some light **rays**. This is how we see color.

The ball looks red. Only red light reflects off it.

All the colors together look white.

The shirt is white. All the colors are reflecting.

The dog looks black. None of the colors are reflecting.

Colors All Around

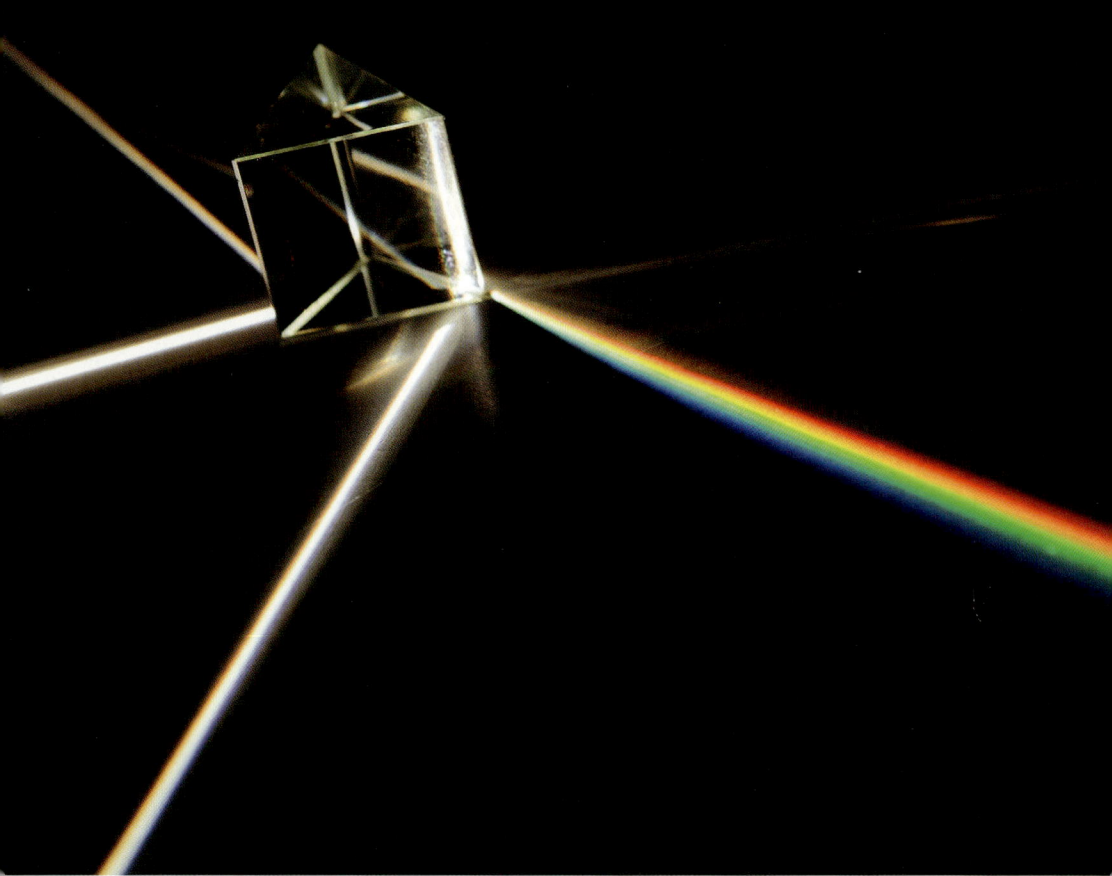

A **prism** separates light colors.

Most prisms are glass or plastic.

A ray of light moves through the prism.

The prism bends the light.
It separates the colors.

A rainbow is bent sunlight.

A **rainbow** shows many colors.

Water in the air reflects sunlight.

The light bends. The colors separate.

Light makes colors all around us.

What colors do you see?

Glossary

colors – parts of light that we see, including red, green, and blue

prism – an object that separates light into colors

rainbow – a curve of colored light in the sky

rays – beams of light

reflects – bounces

Index

lightbulb – 6

prism – 15–17

rainbow – 18

rays – 11, 16

reflect – 9–14, 19

sun – 5

J 535.6 BOO

Boothroyd, Jennifer, 1972-

Light makes colors

OCT 0 3 2014